The Littlest Levine

In memory of my uncle, George Cohen, who conducted the best seders ever—S.L.

For Sean and Mickey—C.K.

KAR-BEN PUBLISHING
A division of Lerner Publishing Group, Inc.
241 First Avenue North
Minneapolis, MN 55401 U.S.A.
1-800-4-KARBEN

Website address: www.karben.com

Library of Congress Cataloging-in-Publication Data

Lanton, Sandy.
     The littlest Levine / by Sandy Lanton ; illustrated by Claire Keay.
         pages   cm
     Summary: Being the youngest in her family means that Hannah cannot do many things, which makes her unhappy, until finally, at Passover, there is a special duty only she can perform.
     ISBN 978-0-7613-9045-9 (lib. bdg. : alk. paper)
     ISBN 978-1-4677-2432-6 (eBook)
     [1. Youngest child—Fiction. 2. Family life—Fiction. 3. Judaism—Customs and practices—Fiction.
4. Passover—Fiction. 5. Seder—Fiction.] I. Keay, Claire illustrator. II. Title.
     PZ7.L293Lit 2014
     [E]—dc23   2013002181

Manufactured in China
1 – PN – 12/29/13

031425K1

The Littlest Levine

Sandy Lanton

illustrated by Claire Keay

KAR-BEN
PUBLISHING

Hannah Levine was little.

She was too little to reach the sink by herself . . .

Too little to tie her own shoelaces . . .

Too little to ride the big yellow school bus with her sister and brother.

"I hate being the littlest Levine!" said Hannah.

"I know," said Grandpa, "but someday you may change your mind."

On Sukkot it was even worse.

Her daddy had to pick her up so she could hang her paper chains from the roof of the sukkah.

"I hate being the littlest," said Hannah.

"Don't worry," said Grandpa.

"Soon you'll be glad to be the littlest Levine."

On Hanukkah, Hannah couldn't light the candles by herself.
Her grandma insisted on guiding her hand.
"I hate being the littlest," said Hannah.

"Be patient," said Grandpa. "Soon you'll be proud to be the littlest Levine."

On Purim, Hannah filled the hamentaschen and folded them up, but her mom had to put them in the oven. "I hate being the littlest!" said Hannah.

"Your holiday is coming, my littlest Levine," said Grandpa. "Let's go into my study, just the two of us. We have a lot of learning to do."

Passover preparations began, and the whole family was busy. But when they cleaned the house, Hannah could only wash the lowest part of the picture window.

When they unpacked the Passover dishes, Hannah could only put the shelf paper in the bottom cabinets.

And when it was time to make the matzah balls, Hannah wasn't allowed near the stove.

But every evening after dinner she and her grandpa went off together.

The afternoon before the seder, Hannah's brother and sister
set the table, her father arranged the food on the seder plate,
and her mother put out the wine glasses.

But once again Hannah and her grandpa disappeared into his study.

When it was finally time for the seder, Hannah put on her new polka-dot dress and a matching ribbon in her hair. She twirled around her room, letting the skirt billow out in a full circle. She was ready.

The candles were lit, and everyone joined in the blessing.
Then they took turns reading from the haggadah.
When it was time for the Four Questions, everyone got quiet.
"Who is the littlest?" Grandpa asked.

Hannah smoothed her hair and cleared her throat. She stood
tall and in her loudest, clearest voice, she chanted:

"*Mah nishtanah halailah hazeh mikol haleilot?* Why is this night
different from all other nights?"

When she had finished reciting all four questions, she sat down.

"My littlest Levine," Grandpa said, "I'm so proud of you."

He gave her a big hug.

"Thank you for teaching me, Grandpa," Hannah whispered.

"Today I love being the littlest Levine."

ABOUT PASSOVER

Passover celebrates the exodus of the Israelite slaves from Egypt and the birth of the Jewish people as a nation. The holiday, observed in spring, begins with a festive meal called a *seder*. Families gather to read the *haggadah*, a book which tells the story of the Jewish people's historic journey from slavery to freedom. Children ask the Four Questions and search for the hidden *matzah* called the *afikomen*. Symbolic foods recall the bitterness of slavery, the haste in which the Jews left Egypt, and the joy of freedom. During the holiday week no *hametz* (leavened food, such as bread) is eaten. Matzah, a flat cracker, takes the place of bread.

ABOUT THE AUTHOR

Sandy Lanton is a former teacher who now writes children's books. Her children's books include *Daddy's Chair* and *Lots of Latkes* (Kar-Ben), *The Happy Hackers* (Wendy Pie Ltd.) and *Still a Family* (Lantern Press). She lives in Plainview, NY with her family.

ABOUT THE ILLUSTRATOR

Claire Keay lives in Rayleigh, Essex, an old market town in the south of England. She works from home in her tiny and very messy studio. Aside from drawing and painting, the great loves in her life are her two sons and breakfast in bed with the Sunday papers.